THE WIND
IN THE
WILLOWS

TREASURY OF ILLUSTRATED CLASSICS ™

THE WIND IN THE WILLOWS

by
Kenneth Grahame

Adapted by
Nicole Vittiglio

Illustrated by
Tim Davis

Modern Publishing
A Division of Unisystems, Inc.
New York, New York 10022

Series UPC: 38150

Cover art by Tim Davis

Contents

The Riverbank

Mole had been spring cleaning all morning. He swept and dusted and painted. He worked until his back ached and his arms were very tired. But spring was in the air outside, and it had made Mole restless. He suddenly threw down his broom and cried, "Forget spring cleaning!" Then he bolted out of his front door. He scraped and scratched upward through the dirt until at last his snout poked out into the sunlight and he was rolling in the warm grass of a huge meadow.

"This is far better than painting," he

said to himself. The sunshine felt hot on his fur, but a soft breeze blew around him. After living underground for so long, he felt like shouting for joy to hear the birds singing. Delighting in the thought of spring without its cleaning, Mole made his way across the meadow until he reached the hedge on the other side.

It seemed too good to be true. All around him birds were building, flowers were budding—everything was happy and occupied. His conscience didn't bother him one bit about all of the housework he had left unfinished. Instead, he felt happy to be the only idle creature among all of the other busy citizens. After all, the best part of a holiday is not really resting yourself, but watching all of the other fellows busy at work.

He thought he could not be happier when, as he wandered along, he suddenly found himself at the edge of a river. He had never seen a river—a sleek and twisting, gripping thing that gurgled and then left with a laugh. Mole was enchanted by the gleams and sparkles, rustles and swirls, chatter and bubble of the great river. He trotted excitedly along the river-bank until he grew tired and decided at last to rest.

As he sat on the grass and gazed across the river, Mole noticed a dark hole in the opposite bank. Something bright and small twinkled down in the

heart of it, vanished, then twinkled once more like a tiny star. Then it winked at him, and so Mole knew that it was an eye peering at him. Slowly, a small face began to grow around it, like a frame around a picture.

It was a brown, round, little face, with whiskers, small ears, thick, silky hair, and with the same twinkle in its eye that had first attracted his notice. It was the Water Rat! The two animals stared at each other cautiously.

"Hello, Mole!" said the Water Rat.

"Hello, Rat!" Mole said.

"Would you like to come over?" Rat asked.

"I suppose there would be no harm in that," Mole said, being new to the riverbank way of life.

Silently, Rat unfastened a rope and tugged at it. He stepped into a little boat, which Mole had not noticed earlier. The boat was the perfect size for two animals. It was blue on the outside and white on the inside. Mole was fascinated by it, even though he did not fully understand its uses.

Rat rowed across the river in no time and helped Mole step gingerly down into the boat. To his surprise and delight, Mole found himself seated in the stern of a real boat!

"What a wonderful day!" he said as Rat shoved off and took the oars again. "I've never been in a boat before in all my life."

Rat could not believe it. "Never been in a boat! What have you been doing, then?" he asked.

"Look ahead, Rat!" cried Mole.

It was too late. The boat hit the bank full force. Rat lay on his back at the bottom of the boat, his feet sticking up in the air. Then he picked himself up with a laugh. "Mole, if you don't have plans for this morning, why don't we go down the river together and make a long day of it?" he suggested.

Mole couldn't think of a thing that would make him happier. He leaned back blissfully into the soft cushions and said, "Let's start at once!"

"Hold on a minute, then!" Rat said. He climbed into his hole and reappeared carrying a huge picnic basket.

"What's inside?" Mole asked.

"There's cold chicken," replied Rat, "and cold tongue, cold ham, cold beef, salad, rolls, lemonade, soda water..."

"This is too much!" Mole squealed.

"It's what I always bring along on these little outings," Rat said.

Mole was charmed by the new life he was about to enter. He trailed his paw in the water and began to daydream. Like the good little fellow he was, Rat didn't disturb his friend.

"I like your clothes, old chap," Rat said after some time had passed.

"I beg your pardon," Mole said, startled out of his daydream. "You must think I'm awfully rude. But this is all quite new to me. So *this* is a river!"

"*The* river," corrected Rat.

"What a jolly life you must lead here by the river," Mole said.

"By it, with it, on it, and in it," Rat said proudly. "It's my world, and I wouldn't want any other. What it lacks isn't worth having. Oh, the times we've had together! No matter the season, it's always full of fun!"

"What's over there?" Mole asked,

pointing to a wooded area near the water meadows on one side of the river.

"That's the Wild Wood," Rat said cautiously. "We riverbankers don't venture there very often."

"Aren't the people who live there nice?" Mole asked a bit nervously.

"Well," replied Rat, "the squirrels are all right. Some of the rabbits are all right, too—but they're a mixed lot. And then, of course, there's Badger. He lives in the heart of the Wild Wood. Nobody interferes with him. They'd better not," he added.

"Who would want to interfere with him?" Mole asked.

Rat hesitated. "There are other types of animals—weasels, foxes, ferrets, and so on. I mean, they're all right sometimes. I'm very good friends with them. But there's no denying that they break out at times. The fact is that they can't really be trusted."

Mole changed the subject. He knew

that it was against animal etiquette to discuss trouble.

"What is beyond the Wild Wood?" he asked Rat.

"Beyond the Wild Wood is the Wide World," Rat said. "But the Wide World doesn't matter to us. I've never been there and will never go there. If you have any sense, you'll never go, either. At last! Here's a nice place to have a picnic lunch!"

They left the main part of the stream and headed into a landlocked lake. On either edge, green grass sloped down and snaky tree roots gleamed below the surface of the water. The beauty of it all was too much for Mole, who held up both forepaws and gasped, "Oh, my! Oh, my!"

Rat tied the boat alongside the bank and helped Mole safely ashore. Then he took the picnic basket out of the boat. Mole begged to be allowed to unpack it, and Rat more than happily let him. While Rat rested, his friend excitedly took the items from the basket, one by one, and gasped, "Oh, my!" at every one. When everything was set out, Rat said, "Dig in, old fellow!" and Mole was very glad to do so.

After some time, Rat noticed that Mole's eyes had wandered. "What are you looking at?" Rat asked.

"I'm looking at a streak of bubbles that is traveling along the water," Mole said. "That's odd."

Suddenly, a glistening snout popped up above the edge of the bank, and Otter lifted himself out.

"Greedy beggars!" he observed. "Why didn't you invite me, Ratty?"

"This was a spur-of-the-moment outing," explained Rat. "By the way, meet my friend Mr. Mole."

"It's a pleasure to meet you," said Otter, and the two animals were friends from that point on.

"The whole world seems to be out on the river today," said Otter. "I came up here to get some peace."

There was a rustle. Suddenly a striped head with high shoulders sprang from a bush behind them.

"Come out, old Badger!" cried Rat.

Badger trotted forward a step, then grunted "Hmm, company!" he said, and disappeared from view.

"He hates society!" explained the disappointed Rat. "We won't be seeing any more of him today. So, Otter, who's out on the river today?"

"Toad's out in his brand new boat," replied Otter. Rat and Otter looked at each other and laughed.

"Whatever Toad takes an interest in, he quickly tires of," explained Rat. "Then he starts on a new hobby and does the same thing all over again."

"He's a good fellow, but he has no stability," remarked Otter.

Just then a boat flashed into their view. It was Toad. The rower was short and stout, and he was splashing rather poorly with his oars. But he was working very hard. Rat hailed him over, but Toad was concentrating on the work at hand.

"He'll tire of the boat very quickly if he keeps splashing like that," Rat said.

"He surely will," giggled Otter.

A Mayfly swerved unsteadily against the current. With a swirl of water and a splash, the Mayfly was gone. So was

Otter. Again, a streak of bubbles swirled across the surface of the river.

Mole knew that, according to animal etiquette, he should not discuss the sudden disappearance of a friend.

"Well," Rat said, "I guess we should get going. I wonder which of us should pack the basket?"

"Oh, please let me," Mole said. So, of course, Rat let him.

Rat rowed gently homeward, murmuring verses of poetry to himself and not paying much attention to Mole. Mole was very satisfied with the events of the day. He already felt at home in the boat. He said to Rat, "Ratty! Please, I want to row, now!"

"It's not as easy as it looks," Rat said with a smile. "You will need to take some lessons before you can row the boat on your own."

Mole thought quietly for a moment. He began to feel very jealous of Rat, who was rowing so strongly and with such ease. Mole felt that he could row just as well. So he jumped up suddenly and grabbed the oars from Rat, who had been daydreaming and was so taken by surprise that he fell backward off his seat and onto his back. Mole took his place and snatched the oars with confidence.

"Stop!" cried Rat from the bottom of the boat. "You'll tip us over!"

Mole swung the oars back with all of his might and made a great attempt at rowing. But he missed the water, his legs flew up over his head, and he landed on top of Rat at the bottom of the boat. He was so alarmed that he tried to grab the side of the boat, but— splash! Over went the boat, and he found himself struggling in the river.

The water felt very cold, and Mole was soaked to the bone. Just when he had risen enough to see the sun shining through the surface, he began to sink again. Then a firm paw gripped

him by the back of the neck. It was Rat, and he was laughing. Rat helped Mole to the shore.

Poor miserable Mole, wet and ashamed, trotted about until he was almost dry, while Rat dove into the water to recover the picnic basket and the boat.

When they had set off again, Mole said in a low voice, broken with emotion, "Ratty, my generous friend! I am very sorry for my foolish, ungrateful behavior. It makes me sick to think that I might have ruined your beautiful picnic basket! Will you overlook it this once and forgive me?"

"That's all right!" Rat said cheerfully. "What's a little wetness to a Water Rat? I'm more in the water than out of it most days. Forget about it! I really think you should come and stay with me for a little while. My home is very plain, but it's comfortable. I'll teach you to row and to swim!"

Mole was so touched by Rat's kindness that a tear came to his eye.

When they got home, Rat gave Mole a robe and slippers. He built a fire in the parlor to warm and dry his friend. Rat told river stories that were thrilling to an earth-dweller like Mole.

"How exciting," Mole cried, his eyes lighting up.

Soon after dinner, Mole became very sleepy. Rat showed him to the best bedroom in the house. As he drifted off to sleep, Mole felt very happy knowing that his new friend, the river, was lapping the sill of his window.

Mole had never dreamed that his life could be so full and so much fun. He hoped that Rat would show him everything there was to see and do on the river.

This was for Mole the first of many wonderful days. As the summer went on, the days grew longer and more interesting. Mole learned to swim and to row. He had become part of the joyful river life. If he listened closely, he could hear the wind whispering in the willows. He felt that it was calling to him, inviting him into an enchanted world where anything could happen.

CHAPTER 2

The Open Road

One bright summer morning, Rat sat on the riverbank, singing a song that he had just composed. He was proud of it, and paid more attention to it than to Mole. He had spent the whole morning swimming with his friends, the ducks, and his song was about them.

"I don't think that I like that song, Rat," Mole said cautiously. Mole was very honest.

"The ducks don't, either," replied Rat with a chuckle.

"Would you please do me a favor,

Ratty?" Mole asked suddenly. "Will you please take me to call on Mr. Toad? I've heard so much about him, and I do so want to meet him."

"Certainly," said the good-natured Rat, jumping to his feet. "We'll paddle up there immediately. Anytime is a good time to call on Toad. He's always glad to see you and always sorry when you leave!"

"He must be very nice," remarked Mole. He got into the boat and took the oars. Rat settled himself comfortably in the stern.

"He is, indeed," Rat answered. "He is quite good-natured and very affectionate. It's true that he is a bit muddled, and at times he can be rather conceited. But Toady also has some great qualities. I just wish he were not so proud of them."

Just then, a dignified old house of red brick with a well-kept lawn came into view. "There's Toad Hall," Rat

said. "The stables are to the right, and the banquet hall is straight ahead. Toad is rather rich, and this is one of the best houses around. But we'd never admit that to Toad."

They passed a large boathouse. They saw many lovely boats, but none of them were in the water. The place was deserted and seemed to have been unused for quite some time.

"I see that Toad has grown weary of boating," observed Rat. "I wonder what new fad he has taken up. I am sure that we will hear about it soon enough!"

They went ashore and strolled across the lawn in search of Toad. They found him resting in a wicker garden chair, a big map in front of him, which he was studying closely.

"Hooray!" he cried, jumping up to greet his visitors. He shook Rat's paw and then Mole's paw without being introduced to him.

"I was just about to send for you,

Ratty," Toad said. "What can I get for you fellows? Come inside and have something!"

"Let's sit quietly for a bit, Toady!" Rat said. Rat threw himself into an easy chair, while Mole took the chair next to him and complimented Toad on his delightful home.

"It's the finest house on the river," Toad boasted, "or anywhere else, for that matter."

Rat nudged Mole. Toad saw him do

it and blushed. An awkward moment
of silence followed. Then Toad burst
out laughing. "All right, Ratty," he
said. "It's my way, you know. Now let's
get to business. I need your help!"

"I suppose you want me to coach
you in your rowing," Rat said.

"Oh, pooh!" Toad said. "Rowing is a
childish amusement. No, I've discovered the only hobby worth having.
Follow me, dear Ratty, and your friend
also, to the stable yard. You shall see
what I am talking about!"

Rat followed, frowning. Parked outside the coach house stood a gypsy
caravan, painted yellow with green
and red wheels.

"Now there's real life, embodied in
that little cart," Toad exclaimed. "Here
today and off tomorrow—the open
road, the dusty highway, towns and
cities! The whole world is before you,
and the horizon always changes! This
is the finest cart ever built—with no

exceptions. Come inside and have a look!"

Mole was very excited, and eagerly followed Toad inside the caravan. Rat stayed outside the cart and snorted as he thrust his hands into his pockets.

Inside the cart Mole saw little sleeping bunks, a table that folded up against the wall, a stove, shelves, a bird in a cage, pots, pans, jugs, and more. It looked indeed very compact and comfortable.

"It has everything that you could possibly want!" said the triumphant Toad. "As we start our journey this afternoon, you'll find that nothing has been left out."

"I beg your pardon," Rat said, "but did I hear you say something about 'we' and 'start' and 'this afternoon'?"

"Come now, dear old Ratty," Toad said imploringly. "You simply must come. I can't manage without you. So consider it settled. You can't possibly stick to your dull old river all of your life and just live in a hole and a boat. I'll show you the world!"

"I'm not coming, and that's final," said Rat. "I am going to stick to my old river and live in a hole and a boat. Furthermore, Mole's going to do as I do, aren't you, Mole?"

"Of course," said the loyal Mole. "I'll always stand by you, Rat. But it does sound as though it might be fun." Poor Mole! The adventurous life was new and thrilling to him, and this trip sounded tempting.

Rat knew what Mole was thinking. He hated to disappoint people, and he would do almost anything to please Mole. His opinion began to change. Toad watched both of them closely.

"Let's discuss it over lunch," Toad suggested. "We don't have to decide in a hurry. Of course, I don't care either way. I just want to make you fine fellows happy."

Lunch was excellent. While they ate,
Toad tried to tempt Mole. He described
the trip they would take and the joys
of the open road. Mole could hardly sit
still, he was so excited. Before long,
the trip was agreed upon. Rat could
not bear to disappoint his friends, so
he decided to go along.

The triumphant Toad asked his
friends to fetch his old gray horse. The
poor horse, without even being asked,
had been chosen by Toad to do the

dustiest job on this dusty expedition.

After Toad loaded the cart with even more cargo and the horse was harnessed, they set off. It was a golden afternoon. Thick orchards lined both sides of the road. Birds whistled to them happily, and passersby waved and wished them, "Good day!"

After they had traveled many miles from home, the tired but happy companions stopped in a meadow. They let the horse graze and ate their dinner in the grass beside the cart. Toad boasted about all he was going to do in the days to come. Before they knew it, the sky shone with stars and a yellow moon appeared from out of nowhere. When they had climbed into their bunks, Toad said, "Isn't this the life? Stop talking about your old river!"

"I never talk about my river," replied the patient Rat. "But I think about it all the time," he added in a lower voice.

Mole felt sorry for his friend. "Do you want to run back to our dear old hole on the river?" he asked. "I'll do whatever you like, Ratty."

"Thank you, but we'll stick it out," whispered Rat. "Toad wouldn't be safe on his own. The trip won't last long. His fads never do."

The end of Toad's fascination with the cart was nearer than Rat suspected.

Toad slept so soundly that no amount of shaking could get him out of bed in the morning. So Mole and Rat took care of the morning duties. Rat fed the horse and cleaned up the last night's mess, while Mole walked to the nearest village, which was very far off, to get some milk and eggs. All of the work was already done by the time Toad woke up.

As they rode along the road, Mole sat up front talking to the horse. Rat and Toad enjoyed the scenery. Then they heard a faint hum in the distance. Glancing back, they saw a small cloud of dust speeding toward them.

A loud popping sound came from the dust cloud. In an instant, a blast of wind forced them to jump into the nearest ditch. It was a motor car! The driver clung tightly to the wheel. Just as fast as it had come upon them, it disappeared in the distance ahead of them, leaving the sound of "poop-poop" trailing behind.

The old horse reared and drove the cart backward into the ditch at the

side of the road. With an awful crash, the cart, their pride and joy, lay on its side, destroyed.

Rat jumped up and down in the road. "You scoundrels!" he shouted, shaking both fists. "You road hogs! I'll report you to the police!"

Toad sat down in the middle of the dusty road and stared in the direction of the disappearing car. At times he faintly murmured, "Poop-poop!"

Mole calmed the horse. When he went to inspect the cart, he found the windows smashed and a wheel missing.

Rat tried to help him, but they were not strong enough to turn the cart upright. "Toad!" they cried. "Come and lend a hand!'

Toad never answered or moved from his spot in the road. They went to check on him and found him in a trance, a happy smile on his face.

"What a glorious sight!" Toad said.

"Poetry in motion! That is the real—the *only*—way to travel! And to think I never knew!"

"What should we do with him?" Mole asked.

"There is really nothing we can do," replied Rat firmly. "He is possessed by his new craze. Let's see what we can do about the cart."

But the cart would travel no longer. Rat grabbed the birdcage and the horse's reins. "Let's go!" he said grimly to Mole. "It's six miles to the nearest town, and we'll have to walk."

"What about Toad?" asked Mole as they set off.

"Oh, bother Toad," Rat said angrily.

They had not traveled far when they heard Toad running up to them. He thrust a paw through each of their elbows. He was out of breath.

"As soon as we get to town, you must report that car to the police," Rat instructed Toad. "Mole and I will go to an inn and find comfortable lodgings."

"Police! Report!" murmured Toad dreamily. "I would never complain about that beautiful car. Oh, Ratty, I am so grateful to you for coming on this trip! If we hadn't come, I might never have seen that car."

"He's quite hopeless," Rat said to Mole. "I give up—when we get to town we'll catch a train that will take us

back to the riverbank tonight."

When they reached the town, they left the horse at an inn stable and hopped on a train that left them very near Toad Hall. They escorted Toad to his door and told his housekeeper to feed him and put him to bed. Then they rowed their little boat down the river toward home.

The next evening Mole was sitting on the bank fishing when Rat came by. "Heard the news?" he asked, shaking his head. "Toad has ordered a large and expensive motor car."

CHAPTER 3

The Wild Wood

For a very long time, Mole had wanted to meet Badger. Everyone knew Badger, or knew of him. Although he was rarely seen, he seemed to have great influence on all of the animals.

Rat always avoided the subject of a visit. "Badger'll turn up someday or other, and then I'll introduce you," Rat would say.

Mole was disappointed. "Why don't you invite him for dinner?" he asked.

"He wouldn't come," replied Rat. "Badger hates society, and invitations, and that sort of thing."

"Then why don't we call on him?" Mole asked.

"He wouldn't like that at all," Rat said, quite alarmed. "He's very shy. Besides, it's out of the question because he lives in the middle of the Wild Wood."

"You told me that the Wild Wood was safe," Mole said.

"It is," replied Rat. "But it is a long way from the river."

For a long time Mole had to settle for this answer. It wasn't until summer was long past that he got his big chance. During the winter, Rat went to bed early and woke up very late. So Mole had a lot of time to himself. One afternoon, while Rat was asleep, Mole decided to explore the Wild Wood on his own and maybe even introduce himself to Badger.

It was a very cold afternoon when Mole slipped out of the warm parlor and into the Wild Wood. At first, everything seemed all right. Twigs crackled under his feet, and funguses on stumps looked like figures, but it was all fun and exciting. He made his way deeper into the woods where the trees crouched lower and there was less light. Everything was very still, and dusk quickly advanced on him.

Then the faces began to appear.

It was over his shoulder that he first thought he saw a face. It appeared to be a small face peeking out at him from a hole. When he turned to look at it, the face disappeared.

He started to walk more quickly and told himself not to imagine such things. He passed another hole, and another, and another, and then—yes— he definitely saw another narrow little face with hard eyes. In an instant, it was gone. He hesitated and walked on. Suddenly, every hole was filled with a face. There were hundreds of them— coming and going rapidly. They all fixed their sinister glances upon him.

He thought that if he could get away from the holes, the faces would be gone. He veered off the path and into unexplored places of the wood.

Then the whistling began.

It was very faint and far behind him, but it made him hurry forward. Then the whistling seemed to be very far ahead of him. That made him want to turn back. As he hesitated in indecision, the whistling sound broke out on either side of him. He was surrounded and all alone and very far from help. Night was closing in.

Then the pattering began.

At first he thought falling leaves made the sound because the sound was so slight. Then, as the sound grew, Mole knew that it was the patter of little feet approaching him. Was the sound in front of him or behind him? It grew and it multiplied until it seemed to be closing in on him. As he stood still to listen, a rabbit came running toward him

through the trees. "Get out of here, you fool, get out!" Mole heard him mutter as the rabbit swung around a stump and disappeared down a burrow.

The pattering increased. The whole wood seemed to be running. In panic, Mole began to run, too. He ran over things, against things, and into things. Finally he took refuge in the dark hollow of a birch tree. He was much too tired to run any farther, so he snuggled into the dry leaves and hoped that he would be safe. As he lay there trembling and listening to the whistling and pattering, he experienced the Terror of the Wild Wood!

Meanwhile, Rat, warm and safe, dozed by his fireside. When he woke up, he looked around for Mole to ask him for a good rhyme to finish a verse he had been working on before he dozed off.

But Mole was not there. The house seemed very quiet.

He called, "Moly," but received no answer. When he went into the hall in search of his friend, he saw that Mole's hat and galoshes were missing.

Rat left the house and followed Mole's footsteps directly into the Wild Wood. It was almost dusk when he reached the first row of trees. He looked around anxiously for any sign of his friend. Here and there, wicked faces popped out of holes. He trudged on, anyway, calling out, "Moly! Where are you? It's Rat!"

He searched the wood for another hour. Then, to his joy, he heard a little voice answering his calls. Following the sound, he made his way through the darkness to an old birch tree. Out of a hole in the tree came a feeble voice, saying, "Ratty! Is that really you?"

Rat crawled into the hollow, and there he found Mole, exhausted and still trembling. "Oh, Rat!" he cried, "I've been so frightened!"

"I understand," Rat said soothingly.

"I did my best to protect you. We river-bankers hardly ever come here by ourselves. Besides, there are many things that you need to know before you come here. Passwords, signs, and such. We must start for home while there is still light."

"Dear Ratty," Mole said, "I'm sorry, but I'm simply too tired to move!"

Rat agreed to let Mole rest for a bit. While Mole napped, Rat rested, too, but he was on guard.

When Mole finally woke up, he was in much better spirits. Rat peeked out of the hole to make sure that the coast was clear. To his surprise, the Wild Wood was buried in snow! And the snow was still falling!

"Well, there is nothing we can do," Rat said. "We must take our chances and be on our way."

After a couple of hours, the two friends were hopelessly lost. They sat down on a tree trunk to get their bearings and figure out what to do next. They were tired and bruised and wet from falling in the snow. There seemed to be no beginning or end to the wood.

"It's much too cold to sit here," observed Rat. "Let's head down into that clearing. Maybe there's a cave we can hide in for shelter."

Mole and Rat headed into the clearing. On the way down, Mole took a bad tumble and fell forward on his face.

"Oh, my leg!" he cried.

"You're not having much luck today," Rat said. "You've cut your shin. I'll bandage it with my handkerchief."

"I must have tripped over a hidden branch," Mole said miserably.

As Rat examined the cut, he noticed that it was very clean. He knew that it was not made by a branch but by the sharp edge of something made of metal. He looked around on the ground where Mole had fallen. Suddenly, he cried, "Hooray!"

"What did you find?" Mole asked.

"It's a door-knocker!" exclaimed Rat, who was suddenly very happy.

"So what?" Mole said.

Rat scraped away at the snow until it flew in every direction. Finally they came upon a solid dark green door. with a doorbell on the side. With the help of the moonlight they could see these words painted on the door:

Mole was surprised and delighted. He cried, "Rat, you're a genius!"

"I suggest that you ring the doorbell while I knock on the door with this stick," said Rat.

As they did just that, they heard the faint sound of a deep-toned bell ringing from inside.

MR. BADGER

CHAPTER 4

Mr. Badger

They waited patiently for a long time. Finally, they heard the sound of someone inside shuffling toward the door. The bolt shot back and the door opened very slowly. A pair of sleepy eyes peered out at them.

"The next time this happens, I shall be very angry," said a gruff voice. "Who is disturbing me? Speak up!"

"It's me, Rat, and my friend Mole," cried Rat. "We're lost. Please let us in!"

"Ratty, my dear little man!" exclaimed Badger. "Come in, both of you. Lost in the snow! At this time of night!"

The two animals couldn't wait to get inside the warm house.

Badger had been on his way to bed when he heard the knocking. He was wearing his pajamas and slippers. He shuffled ahead of his visitors, leading the way by candlelight. They walked down a long passage into a central hall. They could see many other mysterious tunnels branching out. Badger flung open a door and led them into a big fire-lit kitchen.

The floor was made of red brick, and a fire burned brightly in the fireplace. Two high-backed chairs faced each other. In the middle of the room stood a long table with a bench on either side. Rows of spotless plates lined the shelves at the far end of the room. From the rafters hung hams, bags of onions, and baskets of eggs.

Badger gave them pajamas and slippers and told them to sit in front of the fire to warm up. He cleaned and bandaged Mole's wound. In Badger's warm and safe home it seemed that the cold Wild Wood was miles away.

The supper that Badger served was fit for a king. After they finished eating, they all retired to the fireplace where they chatted for a long time. Badger said, "Give me some news from your part of the world! How's old Toad doing?"

"He goes from bad to worse," replied Rat gravely. "He had another smash-up last week. He insists on driving himself when he really isn't capable. He refuses to hire a driver!"

"He's been in the hospital three times," added Mole. "And he's had to pay many fines."

"Badger, do you think we should do something?" Rat asked.

But Badger said he could not do anything. No animal is ever expected to do anything active during the off-season. "When the season has changed, we'll talk to Toad seriously and bring him to reason," Badger said. "We'll make him be sensible!"

Since supper had ended, Rat had fallen asleep two or three times, but Mole was feeling quite lively. Since Mole was an underground dweller by nature, Badger's house suited him well. Rat was used to a fresh breeze and found the atmosphere stifling.

"I think it's time for bed," Badger said. Sleep in late tomorrow morning. Breakfast is served whenever you like!"

When the two tired animals came down to breakfast very late in the morning, they found two young hedgehogs sitting at the table eating oatmeal. The hedgehogs rose to their feet respectfully when Rat and Mole entered the room.

"No need to stand," Rat said. "Where have you come from? Did you lose your way in the snow?"

"Yes, sir," said the older hedgehog. "Me and little Billy were trying to find

our way to school, and we got lost. We finally stumbled upon Mr. Badger's door. We knocked because we knew that Mr. Badger was so kind."

"I see," Rat said as he helped himself to some bacon and Mole cooked some eggs. "What's the weather like?"

"Terrible, sir. The snow is quite deep," said the hedgehog.

The doorbell rang loudly. Billy went to the door to see who was there. He returned in front of Otter, who embraced Rat with affection.

"Get off!" Rat said, with his mouth full of food.

"Everyone along the riverbank was quite alarmed because you weren't home all night," explained Otter. "But I knew that Badger would know what had happened."

"Weren't you nervous in the Wild Wood all by yourself?" Mole asked.

Otter's teeth gleamed as he laughed. "Nervous? Never! Fry me some ham, like a good chap."

After Otter had finished a plate of ham and sent for more, Badger entered. He greeted everyone in his quiet way. "It must be nearly lunchtime," he said. "Better have lunch with us, Otter. You must be hungry."

"Yes, I am!" replied Otter, winking at Mole. "Watching these hedgehogs stuffing their faces with ham makes me famished."

The hedgehogs looked timidly at Badger. They were too shy to defend

themselves.

"It's time to go home to your mother," Badger said kindly. "I'll send someone with you to show you the way." He gave them sixpence each and a pat on the head, and they were off.

The others sat down to have lunch. Mole sat next to Badger. Otter and Rat were deep in conversation about river gossip. Mole told Badger how comfortable he felt in Badger's home. "Nothing can get at you once you're underground," he explained. "You're your own master. Things go on up above, and you only bother with them when you feel like it."

Badger beamed. "That's exactly how I feel," he replied. "The only peace is found underground. No weather to deal with. Take Rat. A couple of feet of water, and he's got to move. Take Toad. Suppose a fire breaks out. Where would Toad be then?" Mole agreed, and Badger instantly took a liking to him.

After lunch, Badger lit a lantern and told Mole to follow him. They passed through a long tunnel, into a corridor, and down a narrow passage with many more passages branching off it and rooms on all sides. Mole couldn't believe the size of it all. "How did you do all this?" he asked. "It's remarkable!"

"It would be remarkable," Badger said, "if I had done it. But I only cleaned it out. Long ago, there was a city of people right where the Wild Wood is now. They were powerful people and great builders."

"What has become of them?" Mole asked.

"Who knows?" Badger said. "But when they went, the winds and rains eventually levelled the city. Then the forest began to grow again. In time, our home was ready for us underground animals, and we moved in. Up above us, on the surface, the same thing happened. Then the Wild Wood became populated with all different kinds of animals."

Mole shuddered at the memory of these animals.

"Well," Badger said, patting Mole on the shoulder, "you'll have no further trouble in the Wild Wood. Any friend of mine walks where he likes!"

When they returned to the kitchen, they found Rat pacing in a restless way. The underground atmosphere made him nervous. He had his coat on. "Come along, Mole," he said. "We must leave in the daylight. We don't want to spend another night in the Wild Wood."

"I'll go with you, Ratty," said Otter. "If there's danger ahead, you can count on me to help!"

"Don't worry, Ratty," added Badger. "My passages run very far and lead to the edge of the wood. You can take one of my shortcuts."

Rat was anxious to get back to his

river. Badger led the way through a very long, damp tunnel until they saw daylight peeking through at the end. Badger said good-bye. Then he scattered leaves and wood over the hole to make it look natural again.

The three friends found themselves standing on the very edge of the Wild Wood. Otter took the lead since he knew all of the paths, and they quickly headed home.

As he hurried along toward home, Mole realized that he was happy among the things that he knew best. He liked to be in places that were traveled often. Nature in the rough and unplowed fields might be fine for others, but he decided that he would stick to more pleasant places.

CHAPTER 5

Home Sweet Home

Mole and Rat were on their way home from a long day of hunting and exploring with Otter. As they talked and laughed, the darkness of a cold winter evening closed in on them, and they still had quite a way to go. They stumbled upon a path that was very well cleared, which made walking much easier. They were certain that this path would lead them home.

"I think we're coming to a village," Mole said cautiously. He slowed down a bit. The animals were not comfortable around villages.

"Never mind," Rat said. "At this time of year all of the villagers will be indoors. We'll slip right through without any trouble. We can peek into the windows to see what they're doing!"

Since it was nightfall when they entered the village, all of the villagers were indeed in their homes. Most of the windows at ground level did not have curtains, so Mole and Rat could see right in. They moved from one window to another as though they were going from theater to theater. Suddenly, a cold gust of wind hit them, reminding them just how cold and far from home they were. They hurried along.

Finally, cottages disappeared and they could smell the friendly fields that they knew so well. They trekked along, each silent in his own thoughts. Mole thought a great deal about dinner. Rat walked some distance ahead of his friend and fixed his eyes on the road ahead of him. So he didn't even notice that Mole had suddenly stopped short in his tracks.

Mole had felt something mysterious that made him tingle all over. Those who are not animals do not have such subtle physical senses and would not understand such a feeling. At first the feeling was familiar, although he could not remember what it was. But then it came to him: It was the feeling of home! He knew that his old home, which he had given up for the river life, must be very

near. Since he had left that spring morning, he hadn't given it much thought. But now the memory was very vivid. It was as though his old home missed him and called out to him. The call was so strong that he felt he must answer it.

"Ratty!" he cried excitedly. "Please come back!"

"Come along, Mole!" answered Rat cheerfully, still walking ahead.

"Please stop, Ratty!" pleaded Mole. "It's my old home! It's near. And I must go to it. Please come back!"

But Rat was too far ahead to hear Mole clearly. "We can't stop now!" he yelled. "Whatever it is you've found, we'll come back for it another day." He moved forward without waiting for Mole's reply.

As he stood alone in the road, poor Mole was torn between his friend and his old home. But his loyalty to Rat was very strong. He would never abandon Rat. So, with a heavy heart, Mole trudged down the path after his friend. A huge sob gathered deep inside him.

Mole finally caught up with Rat, who was happily babbling about what a fine supper and fire they were going to enjoy once they got home. He was talking so much that he didn't even notice how miserable Mole was. Finally, though, after they had traveled quite a distance, Rat stopped and said, "You seem very tired, old chap. Let's stop and rest for a moment."

Mole sat pitifully on a tree stump. He tried not to cry, but the sob deep inside him wouldn't go away. It forced its way up to his throat and, before he knew it, Mole was sobbing.

"What's wrong, old fellow? What can I do to help?" Rat asked.

Between sobs, poor Mole managed to say, "We passed my old home back there. I know it's not as cozy as yours, or as great as Toad Hall, or as big as

Badger's house, but it was my very own little house. And you wouldn't turn back when I called out to you. You wouldn't listen. Oh, Ratty, I wanted to go to it and I had to leave it! It was so close, but you wouldn't take one look back. Oh, dear!" He was sobbed even harder now.

Rat gently took his friend's hand. "What a pig I have been!" he said, ashamed of himself.

Rat waited until Mole had calmed

down a bit. Then he got up from where he was sitting and said, "Well, we should be off now!" He moved in the direction from which they had just come, hoping that Mole would follow.

"Where are you going?" Mole asked.

"We're going to find that home of yours," Rat said.

"We don't have to," cried Mole, hurrying after him. "It's getting too late and dark. And think of the riverbank and supper! Oh, I never meant to let you know how I was feeling!"

"Forget the riverbank!" Rat said heartily. "We're going to find your home if we have to stay out all night!"

They headed back to the spot where Mole had sensed his home. After a great deal of searching and sniffing, Rat noticed a change in Mole. The signals were coming through! He walked through a hedge, with Rat close at his heels. Suddenly, and without warning, he dove, and Rat followed him into a very small tunnel. When they reached a spot in which they could stand up straight, Mole lit a match. Right in front of them was a little door with the words "Mole End" painted on it.

At first Mole was very excited to be back in his old house. But once he lit a lantern and could see, he saw that the place was covered with a thick layer of dust. Mole realized how small and shabby his house was compared with Rat's. He instantly regretted bringing Rat there when they could have been

in Rat's warm, comfortable home.

Rat paid no attention. He was busy running around and inspecting the furnishings. "This is a great house," he called out. "It is so compact and well planned. Did you design it? Splendid! I'll build a fire, and you dust the place off a bit. We'll make a jolly night of it!"

Mole cheered up for the moment. Then he remembered that they had not had supper and that there was hardly any food in the house. He didn't want his friend to be hungry. But Rat encouraged him to search the house from top to bottom for food. They found a tin of sardines, a box of biscuits, and a sausage wrapped in silver paper. In the cellar, Rat found something to drink.

"We practically have a banquet," Rat said. "This is one of the jolliest homes I've ever been in. No wonder you like it so much, Mole!"

Finally Rat and Mole settled down at the table to enjoy their supper. Just

as they were about to open the sardine tin, they heard the scuffle of tiny feet outside. Then they heard broken bits of sentences: "All in line . . . clear your throats . . . where's young Bill . . . hold up the lantern, Tommy."

"What's that?" wondered Rat.

"It must be the field mice," Mole said, with a touch of pride. "They go caroling at this time of year. They always make Mole End their last stop. I used to give them hot drinks and supper when I could afford it. This is just like old times!"

Rat and Mole jumped up and ran to the door to have a good look. Ten little field mice stood in a semicircle. They wore red scarves and held their little hands thrust in their pockets for warmth.

"Very nicely done, boys!" cried Rat heartily. "Come on in and warm up by the fire!"

"Yes, please come in," cried Mole eagerly. "Wait a minute! Oh, Ratty—we

have nothing to give them."

"Leave that to me," Rat said. "Are there any shops open at this time of the night?"

"Certainly, sir," replied one of the field mice.

"Then, off you go at once!" Rat said. Rat gave the young field mouse a list of things to buy from the finest shops, a large basket to carry everything in, and coins to pay for it all.

"These fellows act in plays, too," Mole told Rat. "They make them up by themselves. You were in it. Recite a bit for us!" he said to one of the mice.

The field mouse rose to his feet and giggled nervously. His friends cheered him on, but he could not overcome his stage fright. Just then the field mouse with the goods from the store came through the door, staggering under the weight of the basket.

Rat sent everyone off to do some kind of chore. Before they knew it, supper was ready. Everyone was famished and began to eat immediately. As they ate, they talked about old times.

The field mice updated Mole on the local gossip. Rat said very little. He just made sure that everyone had all that he wanted and that Mole did not have to worry about anything.

When the meal was finished, the field mice scampered on their way, wishing Mole and Rat a joyous season. Their jacket pockets were stuffed with food for their brothers and sisters back home. Mole and Rat relaxed by the fire and discussed the events of the day.

Finally, Rat said, "Old chap, I am ready for bed!" He climbed into his bunk and tucked himself in.

Mole also turned in for the night. As he rested his head on the pillow, he looked around the room and saw all of the things that were so familiar to him. He realized just how much it all meant to him. But he knew that he did not

want to give up his new life on the river with all of its enjoyments. The upper world was calling him back to its open air. It gave him a very good feeling to know that he could return to this place whenever he wished, and that it would always feel like home.

CHAPTER 6

Mr. Toad

It was a bright summer morning. The river was flowing, and the hot sun seemed to be pulling everything green from the ground as if by strings. Mole and Rat had been up since dawn polishing, painting, and repairing their boats. They had just finished eating breakfast when they heard a heavy knock at the door.

"Mole, be a good chap and see who is at the door," Rat said.

Mole went to the door and came back with Badger! It was a great honor for Badger to make a call to their house.

"My friends, the time has come," Badger announced solemnly.

"Time for what?" Rat asked.

"Time for whom, you should say," explained Badger. "It is Toad's hour!"

"Hooray!" exclaimed Mole. "We'll teach him to be a sensible Toad!"

"I've heard that another new and expensive car will arrive at Toad Hall this morning," Badger said. "We must be off to Toad Hall to do something about it."

"You're right," Rat said. "We must stop that unruly animal before he does any damage to himself, or to anyone else!"

Badger led the way as they went to set Toad straight. When they arrived at Toad Hall, they found a shiny new car parked outside. It was bright red, Toad's favorite color. Toad opened the door and came out wearing goggles, a cap, and an overcoat. He was eager to

show the car to his friends.

"Hello, fellows!" yelled Toad happily. Then he noticed the stern look on the faces of his friends. Before he knew it, Toad's friends had grabbed him and were leading him back inside.

"What is the meaning of this?" demanded Toad.

"Take those ridiculous things off of him," Badger said to Rat and Mole.

Rat sat on Toad while Mole took off the motor clothes bit by bit. Toad kicked and screamed the whole time. But finally, when the fancy motor clothes had all been removed, Toad began to look embarrassed. Now that he was merely Toad again and not the Terror of the Highway, he seemed to understand his friends' intentions.

"You've ignored all of our warnings," Badger said. "You've squandered the money that your father left you on senseless things. We've let you make a fool of yourself for long enough." He led Toad into another room to talk.

"Talking will never work!" Rat said.

After almost an hour of Badger's scolding and Toad's sobs, they emerged from the room. Toad frowned and looked very gloomy.

"Have a seat, Toad," Badger said more kindly now. He turned to Rat and Mole. "I am happy to report that Toad has realized his mistakes. He has promised to give up cars forever."

"That's very good news," Mole said.

"Indeed," agreed Rat. As he said this, he was sure that he saw a mischievous twinkle in Toad's eye.

"Toad, tell them what you told me," instructed Badger, "Say that you are sorry for what you have done."

There was a long pause. "No!" Toad said suddenly. "I'm NOT sorry!"

"What?" cried Badger. "But you just said that you were sorry."

"I'd have said anything in there," Toad said. "You're so moving, dear

Badger. But, really, I am not sorry."

"Then you don't promise to never drive a car again?" Badger asked.

"Certainly not!" insisted Toad. "I promise that the very first motor car I see, poop-poop! Off I'll go!"

"I told you so, didn't I?" Rat asked Mole, who nodded in agreement.

"Well, since you won't listen to reason," Badger said, "we'll have to try something else. You've often invited us to stay with you. Now we will. And we won't leave until you've seen the light in this situation."

"It's for your own good," Rat said kindly as they carried the struggling Toad up the stairs. "We'll have such fun together!"

"We'll take care of everything," Mole assured him.

"No more incidents with the police," Rat said.

"And no more hospital visits," added Mole cheerfully.

They left Toad upstairs and met to discuss the best course of action.

"This is going to be hard work," Badger said. "But we must see it through until Toad is well."

Each animal took turns sleeping in Toad's room. Toad would arrange the chairs to look like a car and pretend to be driving. Eventually this stopped, but he grew more depressed.

One fine morning, Rat went upstairs to relieve Badger. Toad was still in bed.

Badger warned Rat that he thought Toad was up to something. Toad was behaving too well.

"How are you, old chap?" Rat asked.

After a few minutes, Toad answered, "Thanks for asking. But first tell me how you are. And how are Badger and Mole?"

"We're fine," Rat said. "Mole and Badger are out and won't be back until lunchtime. Don't lie there moping on such a fine morning!"

"Dear Ratty," moaned Toad, "I am too depressed to get up this morning. I hope I won't be a burden to you for much longer."

"I hope not, too," Rat said. "I don't mind the trouble, but we are missing so much of this fine weather."

"I know I am a nuisance," Toad said.

"I'm glad to go through the trouble to make you sensible," Rat said.

"I would ask you to go fetch the doctor," Toad said, "but I don't want you to go to the trouble."

"What do you need a doctor for?" Rat asked.

"You must have noticed," Toad said. "Oh, never mind. Forget that I asked."

"If you really need a doctor, I will go for one," Rat said.

"Maybe you can find a lawyer while you're at it," Toad said. "I really should make out my will."

Rat thought that Toad must be in very bad shape if he wanted a doctor and a lawyer. He rushed out the door, being careful to lock it behind him. He needed to make a quick decision, but there was nobody to consult. Finally, he hurried off to the village to do as Toad had asked.

Toad watched Rat from his window. Then he got dressed quickly, laughing the whole time. He stuffed his pockets with money. Then he tied his sheets into a rope and lowered himself out of the window. He ran off in the opposite

direction of Rat, whistling a merry tune.

When the others returned, they were surprised to find Toad gone. Badger scolded Rat for falling for such a silly prank. "But we're free, and we needn't waste any more time guarding Toad," he said. "But we'd better stay here at Toad Hall for a while. There's no telling if Toad will be brought back at any moment—on a stretcher or by police officers!"

Meanwhile, Toad was very proud of himself for fooling his friends. He

walked briskly along the high road until he reached a town. He came to an inn called the Red Lion and decided to stop in and have a meal.

He was almost done with his lunch when he heard the familiar sound of a car outside. The party that owned the car came into the inn. Toad quietly slipped out of the room, paid his bill, and went outside. He thought surely there would be no harm in merely looking at the car.

As he stood in front of the car, he wondered to himself if the car would start easily. Before Toad knew it, he was in the driver's seat, had started the car, and was speeding along the high road without a care in the world! He felt as though he were in a dream, and did not once think about the consequences of his recklessness.

* * *

The next thing Toad knew, he was in trouble and facing the judge to explain himself.

"The case is quite clear," said the judge. "The scoundrel who is cowering before us has been found guilty of stealing a valuable motor car, endangering the public, and arguing with the police. Mr. Clerk, please tell me the harshest penalty we can impose."

The clerk replied, "One year for theft, three years for reckless driving, and fifteen years for arguing with the police. That's a total of nineteen years. Let's round it off to an even twenty."

"Excellent," said the chairman. "Prisoner, get yourself together. If you ever come back to us again, it will be a lot more serious than twenty years!"

They dragged the handcuffed Toad, protesting and struggling, through the streets. The townspeople jeered and threw carrots at him. Toad hung his head in shame. Finally, they reached a dark dungeon.

Then the jailer threw Toad into the

dungeon and locked him in. Now Toad was a helpless prisoner in the dungeon of the best-guarded castle in all of England! He hung his head in despair, and tears streamed down his cheeks. Poor Toad was, indeed, in a mess.

"Oh, life is so unfair," he wailed. "I wish my friends were here."

But Toad's friends were nowhere in sight, and he was a captive. There was nothing for him to do but wait, and Toad was not good at waiting.

CHAPTER 7

The Piper at the Gates of Dawn

Meanwhile, Mole lay stretched on his back on the riverbank. Although it was after ten o'clock at night, it was still very hot. Mole had been on the river with some friends. When he returned, he found that Rat was still not back from his outing with Otter. Just then, he heard the sound of Rat's footsteps coming toward him.

"Did you stay for supper with Otter?" Mole asked.

"He wouldn't hear of me leaving without supper," Rat said. "But have you heard? Little Portly is missing."

"That child is always running off," Mole said. "I am sure that someone will find him and return him to his parents."

"It's much more serious this time," Rat said gravely. "He's been missing for days. They have searched everywhere, and there is no trace of him. Otter is afraid that Portly has fallen into the river or fallen into a trap. He is watching by the bridge, where he gave Portly his first swimming lesson."

"Rat, we must do something," Mole said. "Let's take the boat out and search for Portly."

"Splendid idea," Rat said.

They rowed all night long, led by the light of the moon. Every few miles they tied the boat to a willow and searched the hedges, trees, and ditches.

Then the moon began to sink down toward the earth, and dawn began to break. A wind kicked up, and the reeds began to rustle. Suddenly, Rat

heard a beautiful piping sound. Mole continued to row. Rat was simply spellbound by the sound he heard.

"Row on, Mole," Rat said. "The call of that sweet music must be for us!"

"I don't hear anything," Mole said.

"It's getting clearer," Rat said. "Surely you must hear it now."

Mole stopped rowing as the piping caught his attention at last. Except for the marvelous piping, all was still. They had never seen the roses so vivid or the meadow so sweet-smelling.

In the middle of the water they noticed an island. They docked the boat at the flower-lined bank of the island, which was also lined with trees of every kind whose branches were filled with birds.

"Surely we will find Portly here," whispered Rat.

Suddenly Mole felt a great sense of awe, as if someone very important were close by. He noticed that Rat was trembling. All was silent, and the light grew brighter and brighter.

When they looked up, Rat and Mole were astonished by what they saw. A huge beast was looking down at them. He had horns and a hooked nose. One of his shaggy limbs held a pipe that had made that magnificent music. Between its hooves lay Portly!

All at once, the sun rose over the horizon and blinded them. When the two animals were able to see again, the vision was gone, and the only sound that filled the air was the song of the birds chirping.

Mole rubbed his eyes and stared at Rat, who looked around puzzled. The creature had made them forget all of the strange things they had seen. The last thing Rat and Mole remembered was arriving on the island.

When Portly woke up, he was delighted to see his father's friends. Then he started to cry because he felt that he had lost something, but he couldn't quite remember what.

While Mole comforted Portly, Rat noticed some hoof prints in the sand. He wanted to investigate, but then he remembered poor Otter, who was still waiting by the bridge. They loaded Portly into the boat between them and set off. They soon returned Portly safely to his parents.

"I feel very tired," Mole said. "I feel as though I have been through something very exciting and terrible, yet

nothing has really happened."

"I feel the same way," Rat said.

"I still hear that faraway music," observed Mole drowsily.

"Me, too," Rat said. "I hear it, but then it disappears, and all that is left is the sound of the wind in the reeds. Wait! Now it is back again."

The two friends sat and listened to the music for some time. They could hear someone singing. "Look upon my power in the helping hour . . . then you

shall forget . . . helper and healer, I cheer."

"What do the words mean?" Mole asked.

"I do not know," replied Rat.

Then, with a smile on his face, Rat fell fast asleep. Neither Rat nor Mole ever thought of the episode again.

CHAPTER 8
Toad's Adventure

When Toad realized that he was in a dark dungeon, he knew that this grim medieval fortress stood between him and the happy light of day. He also knew that it was unlikely that he would be able to travel the roads of England ever again.

In despair, he threw himself to the ground and began to cry. He had lost all hope. He thought about how stupid he had been to steal that car. For many weeks Toad refused to eat, even though the jailer, knowing that Toad had a great deal of money, offered to

arrange for certain luxuries.

The jailer had a good, kind-hearted daughter. Often, she helped her father with his tasks. She couldn't bear to see poor Toad getting so thin. So she convinced her father to let her be Toad's caretaker.

One day, the jailer's daughter went to see Toad. "Cheer up," she said. "I have brought you some dinner, hot from the oven."

The delicious aroma of cabbage filled

the cell. But Toad was too miserable to eat, so he continued to kick his legs in anger for some time. The jailer's daughter left him alone for a while. After she had gone, the wonderful aroma lingered. It cheered Toad. He began to hope that his friends would find a way to help him.

The girl returned with hot tea and buttered toast. Toad could not resist. He began to sip the tea and nibble the toast. He dried his eyes and started talking about himself and his house and how important he was to the people who knew him. The girl could see how much good it was doing for Toad to talk about himself.

"Toad Hall sounds beautiful," she said with delight.

"It is simply magnificent," boasted Toad. Toad's spirits were restored.

After that, they had many more interesting conversations. With each day, the girl grew sorrier for Toad. Being so vain, Toad mistook her sympathy for love. He even pitied her, because she wasn't very pretty. They were not in the same league, in Toad's opinion.

One morning the girl said, "I have an aunt who is a washerwoman."

"That's nothing to be ashamed of," Toad said.

"Let me finish," said the girl. "You talk too much, and that's a big part of your problem. I have a plan. When my aunt comes to drop off the laundry tomorrow, she will give you her dress and apron. This way you can escape unnoticed. You are very alike in many ways, particularly your figure. I think she would do this for a small fee. After all, you are rich and she is poor."

"Thank you," said Toad, "but you don't really expect the great Toad of Toad Hall to walk around dressed as a common washerwoman, do you?"

"You ungrateful animal," said the girl with disgust. "Then you can just stay here forever!"

Toad felt ashamed. Despite his faults, Toad was honest and always willing to admit he was wrong. He thanked the kind girl and asked her to make the arrangements with her aunt.

The next evening, the plan was carried out. The aunt gave Toad a dress and an apron in exchange for a few gold coins. She asked that she be gagged and tied up to pretend that she was robbed of the clothing. Then she wouldn't lose her job. Toad liked this suggestion because he would be leaving a legend behind!

After the girl and her aunt had helped Toad into the dress, the girl giggled and said, "You're the very image of my aunt, only I'm sure you never looked half so respectable. Now, goodbye and good luck."

So Toad set off with a trembling heart but a firm footstep. After walking through endless courtyards, he finally passed the huge front door and found himself in the fresh air of the outer world! He was free!

Toad walked toward the nearest town, not knowing what his next move would be. Then he saw some red and green lights and heard engines. He was approaching a railway station. Just what I need, he thought.

He went to the station to buy a ticket to the stop nearest to Toad Hall. But when he went to reach into the pocket of his coat, he realized that he was wearing a dress! An impatient line started to form behind him. Horrified, he remembered that he had left his coat, wallet, keys, watch, and money behind in the prison.

"I've left my wallet at home," he said to the clerk. "Please give me a ticket and I will send the money tomorrow."

The clerk just laughed and asked him to step aside. Worse still, the clerk addressed him as "good woman," which angered Toad!

It was hard for poor Toad to have found a way home yet have no money or friends to help him. His escape would be discovered soon, and he would be captured. Toad began to cry. Just then the engine driver noticed him.

"Hello, ma'am!" said the engine driver. "What's the problem?"

"I have lost all my money," Toad said. "I am a poor washerwoman and I can't pay for a ticket. I must get home tonight! My children will be hungry."

"Let's make a deal," said the driver. "My wife is tired of washing my shirts. If you will wash a few shirts for me when you get home, you can ride for free."

Toad agreed and happily climbed up into the cab. Toad knew that he couldn't wash shirts properly, but he would send the driver enough money to cover the cost once he got home.

At last the train began to move out of the station. As the train moved faster and faster, Toad knew that he was getting closer and closer to Toad Hall. Soon he would have good food, a warm bed, and the company of friends. He was so giddy with happiness that he started to skip around.

They had covered many miles when Toad noticed that the driver looked puzzled. He was leaning over the side of the engine and listening to something. Then he climbed on top of the coals to get a better look.

"That's strange," said the driver. "This is the last train running tonight, but I hear another train behind us."

Toad stopped his silly skipping at once. He became very agitated when he thought about who might be on the train behind them.

Then the driver called out, "I can see it! Another train is chasing us at a very high speed! The engine is crowded with police officers and wardens. They want us to stop!"

Toad fell to his knees sobbing. He

begged the driver, "Please save me! I confess. I am not a washerwoman, and I have no children. I am the well-known Mr. Toad of Toad Hall, and I have just escaped from prison! If those fellows recapture me, I'll have to go back to the miserable dungeon!"

The driver asked, "What were you in prison for?"

"Nothing much," said the blushing Toad. "I only borrowed a car while its owners were at lunch. I didn't mean to steal it, really."

The driver looked sternly at Toad. "You have done a wicked thing. I should hand you over," he said. "But you are in distress, and I won't desert you. The sight of an animal crying always gets to me! Don't worry. You'll see. We'll beat them!"

Together they piled more coals into the furnace. The engine leaped, but the other train was still gaining on them.

The driver sighed. "Toad," he said, "I am afraid this won't work. There's only one thing to do. I will go full speed through that tunnel up ahead. The police will slow down for fear of running off the track. Once we are through the tunnel, I will put the brakes on as hard as I can. Then you will jump off into the woods. Hide in the woods before they get through the tunnel and are able to see you. Then I'll go full speed again."

And that's exactly what they did! Toad jumped off and rolled into a mound of leaves. Luckily, he wasn't hurt, so he picked himself up and scampered into the woods to hide.

He peeked out and saw his train speeding away. Then the other train burst through the tunnel, still chasing the first train. Toad laughed.

But when he realized how late and cold it was, he stopped laughing. He was in a strange place and had no money. He didn't want to leave the shelter of the trees, so he went into the woods.

He found the creatures of the woods to be harsh and unfriendly. An owl swooped too close and brushed his shoulder with its wing. A fox passed and made fun of him for being a washerwoman. Finally, he was so tired, hungry, and cold that Toad decided to make a bed of leaves for himself in the hollow of a nearby tree. There he fell fast asleep.

CHAPTER 9

Wayfarers All

It was the height of summer, and some of the greens were starting to turn gold, while some of the trees were reddening.

Rat felt restless and did not know why. He decided to take a walk. All around him animals flitted about. The field mice were digging and tunneling.

"Here comes Ratty," they cried when they saw him. "Help us out!"

"What are you doing?" Rat asked. "It's much too early to start building winter homes."

"Oh, yes, we know," replied the mice.

"But we like to begin early and get the best places. We're making a start."

"Forget about starts," Rat said. "Let's go for a row or a stroll."

"Maybe some other time," said the mice, "when we have finished."

Rat walked away. He felt grumpy. He went back to his river, which never packed up or moved into a winter home. He spotted a yellow bird in the trees. It was joined by another, and then another. Soon there were many birds sitting in the trees.

"Heading south already?" Rat asked. "What's the hurry?"

"We're not leaving yet," called the first swallow. "We're simply making our plans and mapping our route."

"If you have to leave your home and friends," Rat said, "why pretend you're happy about it? Why talk about it sooner than you have to?"

"You don't understand," said one of the swallows. "We feel a sweet unrest

that urges us to move on each year at this time."

"Couldn't you stay just this one year?" Rat asked sadly. "We'll all make you very comfortable."

"I tried to stay one year," said another swallow. "But the air was so cold and the days were so dark. There were no insects in sight. I had to fly through snowstorms to reach the sun again. Now I always heed the call!"

"Ah, yes, the call of the south," said

the other swallows dreamily.

"Why do you bother to come back, then?" Rat asked curiously.

"In due time we get the opposite call, too," said the first swallow.

"We get homesick for the water lilies," added the second swallow.

Still restless, Rat wandered off. Suddenly, he was very curious about the unknown. Gazing south, he wondered what sun-bathed coasts were out there waiting to be discovered. What quiet harbors had he never seen?

He heard the sound of footsteps coming toward him. Rat looked up to find a dusty Sea Rat coming down the road. The wayfarer saluted Rat. Smiling, he turned and sat down in the grass. He looked very tired. He was lean and wore gold earrings. His pants were worn and patched. He carried his belongings in a blue cotton handkerchief.

"I can sense that there is a river close

by," said the wayfarer. "And I can see that you are a mariner. It must be a good life you lead!"

"Yes, it's the only life to lead," Rat said dreamily.

"Not exactly," replied the stranger. "I tried it for six months. It was good, but I got the call to go back to my old life."

"Where do you come from?" Rat asked.

"A nice little farm," replied the stranger. His eyes were focused on the horizon.

"You are not one of us," Rat said. "You are not even from this country."

"You're right," replied the stranger. "I come from a far-off place called Constantinople. I am a seafarer."

"You must go on many great voyages," Rat said. He liked the stranger. "Do you spend months at sea with food and water running low?"

"No, that kind of life would never do for me," said the Sea Rat. "It's the great life of the ports that I love."

"Tell me about your travels," said the Water Rat. "Today, my life seems very limited."

"My last voyage landed me here," said the Sea Rat. "I started out in a small vessel in Constantinople. We went from harbor to harbor. We had golden days and balmy nights. I slept during the day and enjoyed music and feasts at night. We passed through Venice—what a fine city." He was silent for a while, and Rat was captivated.

"Isn't life at sea hard?" Rat asked.

"It is for the crew," said the Sea Rat with a wink.

The Sea Rat told more fascinating tales of life at sea and of the beauties of far-off ports. For a time, he said, he led a lazy life among the peasants near the Mediterranean. After many stories, the Water Rat invited the Sea Rat to his hole for lunch.

"That is downright brotherly of you,"

said the Sea Rat. "But could you bring the food out here? I am not fond of going underground."

The Water Rat raced home and packed a lunch basket with all kinds of fine foods. He hurried back and set it before his new friend. After they had eaten and the Sea Rat was no longer hungry, he continued telling stories of his exciting adventures. He had grown tired of sailing the seas and wanted to try life on a quiet farm. The Water Rat quivered with excitement.

"Why don't you come on my next voyage, brother?" the Sea Rat suggested. "Heed the call. One step will take you out of your old life and into a new one."

Then the stranger went on his way. The Water Rat loaded up the basket and walked home. He packed some of his treasured possessions into a satchel. He felt as if he were in a dream. As he was about to walk out

the door, he bumped into Mole.

"Where are you going?" Mole asked as he grabbed Rat by the arm.

"South, with everyone else," Rat mumbled.

He moved forward. Mole was alarmed to see that his eyes were glazed and seemed to belong to someone else. Mole blocked the way and held him down.

Rat struggled for a while, but then he gave up. He lay still and then began to tremble. Mole sat by his side and waited for this strange fit to pass. Finally, Rat fell into a deep sleep.

Mole was very worried, but he tried to take his mind off of his friend's strange behavior by doing household chores. When he returned to the parlor, Rat was where he left him, sitting awake and silent. His eyes had returned to normal.

Rat tried his best to explain what had happened, but he could not. The spell was broken, and the enchantment had ended.

Mole began to talk casually about harvests and wagons and everyday things. Slowly, the joys of their cozy home life came back to Rat. He joined in the conversation. Mole fetched a pencil and some paper.

"It's been a long time since you've written any poetry, Ratty," Mole said.

Soon Rat was writing poems, deaf to the world around him. Mole felt happy to see that Rat was settling down to his old self.

CHAPTER 10
The Further Adventures of Toad

The sun streamed into Toad's tree hollow very early in the morning. He had been dreaming of Toad Hall. He awoke, sat up, rubbed his eyes, and wondered where he was. Then he recalled everything. How happy he felt to be free!

Toad combed the leaves from his hair and headed off into the woods once again. He wished that he had someone to talk to. As he marched along a canal's edge, a barge towed by a horse appeared. Its only occupant was a large woman wearing a bonnet.

"Good morning, ma'am!" she called to Toad.

"It would be, ma'am," Toad said, "if I weren't in such trouble. My married daughter asked me to come out here. So I left all of the little ones at home, and they're quite mischievous. I've left my laundry business unattended. And who knows what my older daughter might be going through!"

"Where does your daughter live?" asked the barge woman.

"She lives near a grand place called Toad Hall," Toad answered. "Have you heard of it?"

"I'm going that way myself," said the woman. "I'll give you a lift!"

What good luck I have, thought Toad, puffing himself up. I always come out on top!

"The washing business is a very good business to be in," said the woman as they glided along.

"Finest business in the country,"

boasted Toad. "I do all the work myself! I love it."

"What good fortune it was, my meeting you," said the woman.

"Why is that?" Toad asked nervously.

"I like washing just as you do," began the woman. "But my husband is always away. He leaves me to run the barge. Today he is off with his dog, hunting for dinner. I never have time for laundry."

Toad tried to change the subject, but the woman kept talking. "I can't think of anything but my wash," she said. "Would you be so kind as to go in the cabin and fetch some of my laundry? You'll also find a bucket and soap. I'll know you'll be happy doing something that you love!"

"Let me steer," said the worried Toad. "This way you can do your wash the way you like."

"It takes a lot of practice to steer a barge properly," laughed the woman. "Besides, it's boring, and I want you to be happy."

Toad was cornered, so he gave in. Any fool can do wash, he thought. He tried to remember how he had seen other people do it when he had glanced into their windows.

A half hour passed. With each minute of washing, Toad grew more cranky. His back hurt, and his fingers were starting to get crinkly. He lost the soap in the bucket fifty times! A sudden burst of laughter made him turn around.

"I've been watching you the whole time," laughed the woman. "I knew from the beginning that you were a humbug. I knew it from the way you boasted. I'll bet you never washed anything in your life!"

Toad's temper boiled over. "You common barge woman," he yelled. "How dare you talk to your superior like that? I am the well-respected Toad and I will not be laughed at by you!"

"Why, you are Toad!" said the woman

as she took a closer look. "I will not have a nasty, slimy toad on my clean barge!" She grabbed Toad by the legs and flung him overboard.

Toad hit the water with a loud splash. Although the water was cold, it did not cool the heat of his temper. He splashed to the surface and looked back to see the woman laughing at him. Oh, how he wanted to get even with her!

When he reached the shore, Toad rested for a few moments to catch his breath. Then he ran as fast as he could toward the barge, thirsty for revenge.

The woman was still laughing at him. He ran swiftly, untied the horse that was pulling the barge, and jumped on its back. When he looked back, Toad saw that the barge and the woman had run aground.

After galloping a long way, the horse stopped to nibble some grass. Toad

looked around. He was in a large
meadow near him was a gypsy caravan.
A man sat next to it. A fire burned close
by, and Toad smelled the aroma of delicious food cooking. Now he was really
hungry. He wondered if it would be
more effective to fight the gypsy or to
sweet-talk him to get some food.

"Do you want to sell that horse?"
the gypsy asked.

At first Toad was surprised. But
then he realized that the horse could

get him money and a hearty breakfast.

"That's out of the question," he said. "I would never sell this beautiful creature. This horse is a prize Hackney. But what's your offer?"

"A shilling a leg," replied the gypsy.

Toad counted on his fingers to get the total. "That's four shillings," he said. "That's not enough."

"I'll make it five," said the gypsy. "That's my final offer."

To one in Toad's situation—with no

money, no food, and being far from home—five shillings should be enough. But not for Toad. He said, "Give me six shillings and as much breakfast as I can eat, and it's a deal."

The gypsy grumbled, but in the end, he gave in. Toad snatched the money and ate all of the food that the gypsy supplied—he ate and ate and ate! Then he said good-bye to the gypsy, bade farewell to the horse, and headed in the direction the gypsy told him. He felt strong and confident now.

As Toad ambled along, he thought about the events that had led to his current predicament. He said to himself, "Surely, I am the most clever Toad in all the world. I am handsome, popular, and successful." He was quite full of conceit. But his pride was once again about to be greatly wounded.

After walking miles through country lanes, Toad finally reached the high road. As he turned into it, he saw speeding toward him a speck that became a dot and then a blob. A horn sounded a warning, and Toad was soon twirling around with joy. "This is real life again!" he shouted. "Perhaps someone will give me a ride. Imagine Badger's surprise when he sees me arriving at Toad Hall in a car!"

He stepped confidently into the road to flag down the next car. When the car came near, Toad's heart sank. It was the very same car that he had stolen from the Red Lion! He sat down by the side of the road, afraid that he would be arrested again!

The car drew closer and closer, and then it stopped right in front of him. Two men got out. Toad heard one of them say, "What a poor washerwoman! Maybe she is ill. Let's drive her to the next village." They lifted Toad into the car.

Once Toad knew that he had not been recognized, his courage was restored. Cautiously, he looked up.

"How are you feeling, ma'am?" asked one of the men.

"I feel much better," replied Toad. "May I sit in the front seat beside the driver?"

"Of course," said the man as he helped Toad over the seat.

Toad was overjoyed. "Please sir, may I drive for a while?" he asked.

"I like your spirit," said the man. "Go ahead, have a try!"

Toad eagerly took the wheel. He drove very carefully at first. But then he went faster and faster!

"Be careful, washerwoman," the man said.

This made Toad angry! "I am Toad— the car snatcher, prison breaker, Toad who always escapes! Have no fear!" he screamed.

All at once the men rushed at him. "Seize him!" they cried.

They should have thought to stop the

car before they tried to capture Toad! With one swerve of the wheel, Toad sent the car crashing into a hedge. He landed in the soft grass of the meadow. But the car was submerged in a pond, and the men splashed around in the water.

Toad got up and ran off as fast as he could. When he finally caught his breath, he began to giggle. He thought, as usual, I come out on top! What a great Toad I am! How clever I am!

Then he heard a noise. When he turned around, he saw the men running after him!

Toad, too, began to run. He was terrified. How silly I am, he thought. Once again Toad was in trouble.

The men were catching up to him. He tried his best to outrun them, but his legs were short. He struggled on frantically. Suddenly, he found himself under water. In his panic, he had run right into the river!

As he swam, he promised never to

steal or be conceited again. He approached a big hole in the bank. With his paw, he grabbed on to the bank and pulled himself out of the water. For a while, he sat there panting.

Then he saw someone running toward him. With relief, Toad recognized a familiar face—a small, brown face with whiskers and neat ears and silky hair. It was Rat!

Toad breathed a sigh. Finally, a friend had come to save him!

CHAPTER 11

Like Tempests Came His Tears

Rat helped pull the waterlogged Toad from the hole. Although he was covered in mud, Toad was happy to see an old friend at last.

When they arrived back at Rat's home, Toad cried, "Ratty, I've been through such trying times. You couldn't even imagine! I've been in prison—but escaped, of course. I've been thrown in a canal—but I swam ashore! I cleverly fooled everyone. I am a smart Toad. Listen to this . . . ."

"Toad! Go upstairs and clean yourself up and put on some of my old clothes,"

Rat ordered firmly. "Stop boasting and be off!"

At first, Toad wanted to say something back. But when he caught a glimpse of himself in a mirror and saw how horrible he looked, he silently went upstairs to wash. When he finished, he spent a long time admiring himself.

When Toad finally came back downstairs, he found lunch was on the table. While they ate, Toad recounted his adventures to Rat, at every opportunity pointing out his cleverness. The more he boasted, the more silent Rat became.

"Toady, you've been making a fool of yourself!" Rat said. "You've been imprisoned, starved, chased, and insulted. Where's the fun in that? You know you've had trouble with cars since the day you first saw one, yet you still stole one! When are you going to be sensible and think about your friends? Do you think we like to be known as fellows who are friends with a thief?"

One of Toad's good qualities was that he never minded being scolded by a good friend. He always tried to see things from their point of view. So, although he did think that his escapades were fun, he sighed deeply and said, "How right you are, Ratty! I will be good from now on. I am quite done with cars. I was thinking I'd give motorboats a try. But, for now, I am going to lead a quiet life. No more adventures for me! I am going to stroll quietly to Toad Hall."

"Toad Hall!" cried Rat. "Haven't you heard?"

"Heard what?" asked Toad.

"The weasels have taken over Toad Hall," Rat said.

Toad put his head down on the table and began to cry as Rat told the story of the takeover.

"After you muddled things up, the Wild Wood animals said that you had gotten what you deserved," Rat report-

ed. "We riverbankers stood up for you, though. The Wild Wood animals said that you would never come back again. But Mole and Badger stood by you."

Rat continued. "Mole and Badger moved into Toad Hall to get it ready for your return. One stormy night as they sat by the fireplace, ferrets and weasels crept in through the kitchen window and attacked. Mole and Badger tried to fight back, but there were hundreds against them. They were beaten and thrown out into the cold rain. They were called many horrible names!"

At this point the unfeeling Toad actually snickered a bit.

"The Wild Wooders have lived at Toad Hall ever since," Rat said. "They lie in bed all day, eat your food, and make cruel jokes about you!"

Toad's eyes flashed angrily. "I'll take care of that," he said.

"There are too many of them for you," Rat said.

But Toad was already off, marching down the road with a stick in his hand. When he got to his gate, a ferret with a gun popped up out of nowhere.

"Who goes there?" said the ferret sharply.

"Come out at once," demanded Toad, stamping his foot.

The ferret shot at Toad. The bullet whizzed over his head. The startled Toad ran back to Rat's house, crestfallen.

"You'll just have to wait," Rat said. But Toad did not give up so easily. He hopped into Rat's boat and set off for Toad Hall. He was looking longingly at his home when—crash! A huge stone fell from above and made a hole in the boat. He looked up and saw a weasel gazing down at him with glee.

"It'll be *you* next time, Toady," warned the weasel.

Mole ran back to Rat again.

"You lost my favorite boat!" Rat said

angrily. "It's a wonder you can keep any friends at all!"

Toad admitted he was wrong and apologized to Rat. He promised Rat that he would take no further actions without Rat's advice.

"What have Mole and Badger been up to?" Toad asked.

"They have been camping out day and night in all kinds of weather to guard your house," Rat said. "They have been keeping a close eye on the weasels and ferrets. You don't deserve such loyal friends. You'll be sorry you didn't value them more!"

"I am an ungrateful beast," sobbed Toad. "I will go and find them at once. Oh, wait. It is time for supper."

When they had finished eating, they heard a knock at the door. It was Badger. He was covered with mud and looked very tired. He shook Toad's paw. "Welcome home, Toad," he said.

Then Mole came to the door, unwashed and shabby. "Hooray! It's Toad!" he said. "You must have escaped, you clever animal!"

Immediately, Toad swelled with pride. "I'll tell you about my adventures," Toad said, "and you can judge for yourself just how clever I am."

"Toad, do be quiet," Rat said. "And don't encourage him, Mole. Tell us what is going on and what would be best to do, now that Toad is back."

"The situation is very grim," Mole reported. "They have guards posted everywhere."

"I know what Toad should do!" Rat exclaimed.

"No, I do," Mole said.

"I won't be ordered around by you fellows!" cried Toad.

They were all yelling at the same time. Suddenly Badger yelled, "All of you be quiet!"

No one spoke until Badger finished his supper. The animals had great respect for him. When he had finished, he said, "Toad, aren't you ashamed of yourself?"

Toad began to cry.

"Stop crying," Badger said, more kindly. "We'll let bygones be bygones. We can't attack the place. The ferrets are very good guards."

"I shall never see Toad Hall again," Toad sobbed.

"Cheer up," Badger said. "I will tell you a great secret. There is an underground passage that leads from the river right into Toad Hall."

"No, there isn't," replied Toad. "I know every inch of Toad Hall."

"Your father told me about it," explained Badger. "He didn't tell you because he knew that you couldn't keep a secret."

"Well, I suppose I am a bit talkative," admitted Toad. "Being so popular, when I get together with friends, we tell all kinds of witty stories. But never mind.

How is this passage going to help us?"

"I asked Otter to disguise himself as a weasel," explained Badger. "He's been working as a chimney sweep at Toad Hall. He says that there's going to be a banquet tomorrow night. All of the weasels will be there—unarmed! The passage will lead us into the dining hall, and we won't have to pass the guards."

"We'll sneak up on them," Rat said.

"And attack!" cried Toad.

"Our plan is settled," Badger said.

All of the animals got a good night's sleep, especially Toad. By the time he

came down to breakfast in the morning, the others had already finished. Rat was very busy gathering enough weapons for everyone to use in the day's attack.

"We won't need all that," Badger said. "Sticks will do."

"It's better to be on the safe side," Rat replied.

Toad picked up a stick and started swinging. "I'll teach them to steal my house!" he cried.

Mole came tumbling into the room. "I've been teasing the ferrets," he began proudly.

"I hope you've been careful," Rat said.

"I put on Toad's washerwoman dress and went to Toad Hall to ask if they wanted any washing done," explained Mole. "Wasn't that clever?"

Toad felt jealous. He wished that he hadn't overslept. Then he could have done it.

"When they told me to go away," continued Mole, "I told them that it would

not be me running in a short time! 'My daughter works for Mr. Badger,' I said, 'and she told me that hundreds of Badgers plan to attack with rifles tonight!'"

"How could you, Mole! What a stupid thing to say," cried Toad. "You've ruined everything! Toad Hall is lost."

But Badger simply said, "What a clever creature you are, Mole. I have high hopes for you."

Toad was very jealous now. He did not understand what Badger was talking about. Poor Toad could not think of anyone or anything but himself.

After a hearty lunch, Rat resumed gathering his weapons. Mole took the opportunity to lead Toad outside and ask him to tell all about his adventures. Mole was a good listener, and Toad always enjoyed embellishing stories about himself. In fact, much of his story wasn't really fact, but more of Toad's boasting.

CHAPTER 12

The Return of Toad Hall

When it started to get dark, Rat called everyone back into the parlor. He instructed them about how to dress for their mission. Then he handed out all of the weapons he had gathered.

When he had finished, Badger lined everyone up and said, "Toady, be sure not to chatter so much!"

The foursome walked along the river, with Badger in the lead. Everyone walked silently along, except for Toad, of course, who managed to fall into the water with a loud squeal.

Badger was very angry and assured Toad that the next time he made a fool of himself, he would be left behind.

At last they were in the secret passage. It was dark, narrow, and cold. Toad started to shiver. He was afraid to get left behind, so he started to run. He fell into Rat, who fell into Mole, who fell into Badger. At first Badger thought they were being attacked. When he found out the truth, he was very angry. If not for the other two sticking up for him, Toad would have been left behind.

Suddenly they heard the very distant sound of cheering and stamping. They knew that they were near the banquet hall. They hurried along the passage until it ended at a trap door that led up to the pantry. They broke through the door and found themselves right outside the banquet hall. They could hear all of the weasels laughing and mocking Toad.

"Let me at them!" Toad muttered.

"Everyone get ready," Badger said. "The time has finally come!"

When Badger thrust the door open, the challengers heard horrible shrieks. Weasels and ferrets went flying in all directions as they tried to escape. Badger, Mole, Rat, and Toad were only four against hundreds, but the weasels panicked, thinking that the room was full of monstrous Badgers. They fled from Toad Hall in terror.

The attack soon ended. Then the victors set the straggler weasels busy cleaning the place. Toad rummaged some food for his guests. Mole went outside to check, and reported that the coast was indeed clear.

"You're an excellent animal, my dear Mole," Badger said. "I'm very pleased with you."

Although Toad felt jealous of the way that Badger doted on Mole, he thanked Mole. Happily, they finished their supper and went to bed.

The next morning Toad came downstairs very late, as usual. The kitchen was a mess, and he saw Mole and Rat sitting in wicker chairs telling stories and laughing. Badger was reading his newspaper. Toad felt a bit upset about the mess in his house.

"Toad, you really should have a party to celebrate our success," Badger said. "It's expected of you."

"Well, if you really want to have a party in the morning . . . ," Toad began.

"Don't pretend to be more stupid than you really are," Badger said. "The party will be at night. Go off and write the invitations."

"You want me to stay indoors and write invitations?" Toad asked, amazed. "I want to go boast and enjoy myself! But no, I'll do as you ask. Go outside with the others and enjoy yourselves while I toil away!"

While he was talking, Toad got an

idea. He would write the invitations, and he would be sure to mention at the party the starring role he had in the attack! He planned to give many speeches about his bravery. This idea greatly pleased him. When he was finished, he told one of the weasel prisoners to deliver the invitations.

When the others came back into the house, Toad was in a very good mood. When they finished lunch, Toad began to swagger off to the garden, but Rat grabbed him by the shoulders, and he and Badger took the conceited Toad into the other room.

"Look here, Toad," Rat said. "There will be no speeches at this party."

"May I just sing one little song?" Toad asked.

"No," Rat said firmly. Rat did feel a little sorry for Toad when he noticed his lip trembling.

"You must turn over a new leaf sooner or later," added Badger.

Toad was defeated. "All I wanted was one more night of boasting," he said sadly. "But you are right. From now on, I will be a different Toad." With that, he left the room.

"I feel like a bully," Rat said.

"I know," replied Badger, "but it had to be done."

Finally, the hour of the party drew near. Toad was very sad. He got up and arranged the chairs in the room into a semicircle and closed the door.

Then he bowed and started to sing proudly to his imaginary audience. He sang his song over and over again. When he had finished, he went downstairs to greet his guests.

All of the guests cheered when he entered the room. They said that he had been courageous and clever. But Toad gave all of the credit to Rat, Mole, and, of course, Badger. The other animals were shocked by Toad's new attitude. Could this be a new Toad, they wondered.

The party was wonderful. But through all of the laughter and merriment, Toad remained quiet. Some of the animals remarked that things weren't the same as they were in the old days. The guests demanded that Toad make a speech or sing a song. But Toad shook his head and remained silent. He was, indeed, a changed Toad!

After this great incident, the four animals lived their lives in peace and

contentment. Toad sent the jailer's daughter a pretty gold chain and locket. He also compensated the engine driver and even the barge woman for their troubles.

Sometimes during the long summer, the four friends strolled through the Wild Wood. All of their friends greeted them warmly. The mothers of the weasel children would then point and say, "There goes the great Mr. Toad, and the brave Water Rat, and the famous Mole of whom you so often

have heard your father speak!"

But when the children misbehaved, their mothers would say, "If you don't hush up, the terrible gray Badger will punish you!" The mothers knew that when the children heard Badger's name, they were like the animals of the Wild Wood—quiet and respectful. Of course, Badger would never hurt a fly. And though he cared little for society, he was very fond of children.

About the Author

Kenneth Grahame was born in Edinburgh, Scotland, on March 8, 1859. His mother died when he was a child of five. Kenneth and his two brothers and sister went to live with their grandparents in England, close to the Thames River and the Windsor Forest, where this story takes place.

He excelled in school, but his uncle could not afford to send him to Oxford University. Instead, Grahame went to work for the Bank of England. He worked there for many years.

Grahame's real passion was writing. In 1908, he wrote *The Wind in the Willows,* partly as a gift for his young son. His other works include *The Golden Age* and *Dream Days*.

Grahame died in a small town by the Thames River on July 6, 1932.

The Adventures of Pinocchio

Alice in Wonderland

Beauty and the Beast

Frankenstein

Great Expectations

Journey to the Center of the Earth

The Jungle Book

King Arthur and the Knights of the Round Table

Peter Pan

The Prince and the Pauper

Pygmalion

The Time Machine

Treasure Island

White Fang

The Wind in the Willows

The Wizard of Oz